SAINT CLO

The First Christian

France Tells Her Story

BLANDINE MALÉ
HÉLÈNE FABE-HENRIET

Saint Clothilde

The First Christian Queen of France Tells Her Story

Translated by Carlos Grider
Illustrations by Brunor

IGNATIUS PRESS SAN FRANCISCO

Original French edition:
Moi, Clothilde, ou les premiers pas de la France

Cover art: Brunor
Cover designed by Riz Boncan Marsella

ISBN 978-1-58617-473-6
Library of Congress Control Number 2011905246
Printed in the United States of America ♾

Contents

I. Clothilde recalls her youth in Lyon, where her father, Chilpéric, is the king. She imagines her parents, her sister, and others around her. She relives the important events there. 9

II. Clothilde and her mother and sister withdraw to Geneva after the death of Chilpéric. They receive advice from Bishops Avitus of Vienne and Prudentius of Lyon. Young Sédéleube founds a monastery. Clovis, king of the Franks, asks for Clothilde's hand in marriage. Departure of the princess, her voyage, and the meeting with her fiancé. 21

III. The trip to Soissons, Clovis' royal capital. Welcome by Bishops Remigius and Principius. The year 493: marriage. Introduction to a court, the majority of which is pagan. 33

IV. First year of marriage. Clothilde learns what her role as queen will be. She visits peasants, goes on hunts. She attends the burial rites of a warrior. Summer in the royal villa. Meeting with Bishop Remigius. Message from Geneviève of Paris. 43

V. Birth and baptism of Ingomer. Birth of Clodomir. Birth of two more sons and one daughter. Victory over the Alamanni. Clovis promises to be baptized.

Bishop Remigius gives instruction to Clovis. Clovis' baptism in Reims. 53

VI. Clovis' military expedition in Burgundy. Clothilde's trip to Auxerre. A trial. Departure by the army to fight the Visigoths south of the Loire. Victory at Vouillé. Clothilde joins her husband in Bordeaux. A stay in the villa of a noble Gallo-Roman. At Tours, Clovis receives his badges of office as a Roman consul. Clovis chooses Paris for his capital. 65

VII. Clovis and Clothilde in Paris. Their wise government. Construction of the Basilica of the Holy Apostles. Death of Clovis. Division of the kingdom between the three sons. Clothilde withdraws to Tours with her daughter. Clothilde's unhappy marriage to Amalaric in Spain. Vengeance by her brothers. Death of the princess. 77

VIII. The year 524: a terrible year. Murder of Clothilde's grandchildren by their uncles. Clodoald is saved. Clothilde's last return to Tours. She lives the life of a nun. Clodoald, now a hermit, receives a visit from his grandmother. Clothilde's acts of charity. She prays to Saint Martin to keep her sons from warring against each other. She saves a soldier and his family from a life of misery. 89

Epilogue 101

The first queen of the Franks tells her story . . .

In the year 545, the former queen of the Franks, retired and living in the city of Tours, looks back on the great events of her life . . .

Clothilde remembers . . .

I

In the city of Tours, Easter morning of the year 545 . . .

I awake joyous this morning. The heavens are celebrating, and the bells also rejoice by sending, from bell tower to bell tower, their message of the Resurrection. What a delight it is to celebrate Easter one more time—and without doubt, the last, for I am nearing seventy and my strength is waning.

Seated here at my window, I watch the bell towers of the basilica as they emerge from the mist. That is where blessed Martin lies in rest. How I enjoy looking at that place, for it holds the relics of the evangelizer of Gaul, the protector of my sons, kings of the Franks. I had sought refuge near Martin at the death of Clovis, when my human hopes were dashed, some thirty-four years ago.

I founded this convent where I now live like a nun. I have given up silk robes for a tunic of rough serge and choice delicacies for bread and vegetables, the food of the humble. I have vowed my life and my riches to the poor and the ill. Our Lord said, "As you did it to one of the least of these my brethren, you did it to me."

Through wisps of mist I can see the river Loire. I have always loved cities that lie next to water. I was born in Lyon, between the Saône and the Rhône. While still a small child, I was already tugging my nursemaid to their banks, where I would remain motionless for a long time, watching the swirling waters.

Now that I am no longer active, I have all the time in the world to contemplate the river beside which I am nearing the end of my life. And now my spirit is finding peace. If painful memories assail me, I offer them up to the water's course, which carries them off. But on this blessed Easter morn, it is a flood of happy images that I welcome. And they take me back to my most distant past.

I see Lyon again, that dear city where I was born. At the height of the Roman Empire, it was the capital city of the Gauls. But when the empire collapsed, Lyon's walls did not protect it. Sometimes, at the corner of a winding street, one finds the ruins of an imposing monument, the remains of former splendor. Now it is only the capital of my father's kingdom. My family is Burgundian, originating from beyond the river Rhine. Together with other Germanic invaders, we occupied all of Gaul. Our particular territory, located in the southeast of Gaul, is called Sapaudia (Savoy), and my father and my uncles govern it officially in the name of the emperor. But the emperor is no longer in Rome; he is very far away, in Constantinople. In fact Romans living here in Gaul have become our subjects.

But the people of Lyon have no reason to complain, as my father, Chilpéric, is a good sovereign. He protects the humble—something that elsewhere does not happen often. Once, an abbot alerted him that a great landholder had reduced some poor peasants to slavery. My father had them freed immediately.

My father calls me his "very well-behaved Clothilde". Whenever he enters the quiet women's quarters, everything turns lively at the very sound of his hearty voice. He picks me up in his arms, and I am in wonder of him, for no one is as tall or as handsome as he. His red mustache rubs against my cheek. But I do avoid contact with the cold enamel-and-gold clasp that holds his tunic shut. This pin is in the form of a dragon, and a servant has told me that the dragon is a creature of the devil. But papa claims otherwise. He says that in the land from which we come, such animals are everywhere, as are elves, goblins, and fairies. I listen, delighted. Papa makes up wonderful stories, and his joy for life is contagious.

My mother, Carétène, remains in the radiant shadow of her husband, discreet as a wife should be; but her influence is great, and everyone knows it. Besides, among the Germans, women play a more important role than they do among the Romans. Chilpéric and Carétène are a model couple. They are deeply united. The only cause of distress for my mother is that her husband is reluctant to break with his religion,[1] which is different

[1] The Burgundians, like almost all Germans, had converted to Arianism. That heresy denies the divinity of Christ.

from our own. He does not want to upset the Burgundians. But deep in his heart, he is Catholic like his wife and children.

I admire my mother's calm, her serenity, and I follow her everywhere. She goes often to her chapel, where her face is aglow whenever she lifts her eyes toward the holy images. I have sensed the flame that burns beneath the seeming coldness of the queen: she greatly loves Jesus and Mary. It is at her knees that I, too, am learning to love them for the whole of my life. My mother is passing on to me her Catholic faith. But of those in her circle, she is almost alone in rejecting Arianism. She firmly believes that in Christ, God became man because of his love for us. It is a mystery, as is everything that concerns the divine. And I understand that God is both very great and, at the same time, very near to us.

The religious separation with my people grieves me. But I cannot approve of the scorn of Burgundians who flaunt their Arianism only for the purpose of distinguishing themselves from their subjects, who were, after all, Christians long before they were. My mother, my sister, and I pray often for an end to this religious division and for the unity of all the people in the country, no matter what their origin. In doing so, without being aware of it, I am preparing to become, one day, the privileged instrument for the conversion of a people.

While still very young, I used to think about conse-

BRUNOR

crating myself to God. I had learned to pray by observing my mother. I loved the pomp of religious worship, the white and gold vestments of the priests, and above all the singing, which would transport me with pure delight. One of my oldest memories is of a ceremony honoring the martyrs of Lyon, the first witnesses for the faith in Gaul. I can still see myself hanging onto my nursemaid's veil, climbing a hill in a surge of hymns. We plunge into the shadow of an archway and then emerge into the light of the amphitheater. Priests are singing psalms while waves of a delicious scent spread everywhere. It is incense, which I will love always. I pray for little Blandina, delivered over as a martyr to the ferocious beasts.

I was fascinated by the Bible stories that my mother told me, even more than by the stories from my father. As soon as I was able to read, I became engrossed in these stories to the point of preferring them to play. So the chapel and the library were my favorite haunts. My sister, Sédéleube, used to call me "little nun". She was a true tomboy, a whirlwind of laughter and shouting. Yet it was she who left the world to found a monastery. For me, Providence had prepared another role.

I was very eager to learn—as was everyone in my family. My father once said, "Well, the Romans treat us as barbarians, so we shall be educated barbarians!" And then he burst into his magnificent laughter. What exciting hours my sister and I spent together in the quiet library where papyrus rolls were lined up, filled with knowledge. I can still see our tutor, a shy, learned old man. Sometimes Sédéleube would have fun by getting him started on his favorite topic: the discussions between the heretics and Irenaeus, the former bishop of Lyon. Our tutor would then jump up from his stool, wave his arms, roll his furious eyes, and verbally slay the adversaries of the Church. My sister would laugh under her breath, but I would sympathize with our tutor. I grieved with him to see Irenaeus' city in the hands of the Arians.

One day I dared bring up the matter with our bishop named Prudentius, who was often received at the palace. My father knew how influential Prudentius was. In the eyes of the Romans, he was the defender of the city and its patron. On the other hand, my mother revered him for his great acts of charity. I made arrangements to accompany his litter as he proceeded through the gardens. I then asked him the question that was troubling me. "Venerable father, why does God permit the success of Arianism? Why do the German people remain in error?"

The bishop answered, "My child, according to the words of the psalmist, for God, 'a thousand years are as a day.' God is patient, he waits for the conversion of those who have gone astray. It is up to us to pray that this takes place and that the day of the Lord may come." Then, looking me straight in the eyes, Prudentius solemnly added: "However if he has given us high rank in the world, let us be aware that we can be called one day to assist in divine works." Those words and that look have remained engraved in my memory.

I seldom confided in others. I was secretive and, like my mother, reserved. Even with my friends, I did not reveal what was deep in my heart. However, I was very attached to them, and I have remained faithful to them beyond death. They were three. One Roman, Luctérie, and two Burgundians, Gondwina and Brunhilde. We often went on horseback rides with good escorts, as the countryside was not yet secure. Sometimes we strolled in town, guided through the maze of merchant streets by Luctérie. That was a colorful world, where all languages could be heard and where tunics from the south were to be seen alongside the tailored clothing of the north. Whenever a litter passed by, escorted by slaves, we would have fun recognizing, behind the half-open curtains, some senator ending his nap on purple cushions or some great lady bedecked in jewels and trailed by the heavy scent of perfume!

Above all, it was the port that attracted us with all its activity and its different scents, mingled with or dominated by spices. Heavy barges drawn by draft horses were unloaded. We spent a long time watching those that were heading downriver toward the land of the sun.

Brunhilde was my favorite companion. We shared a love of music. She sang beautifully, and I would accompany her. In those days, time was of no importance.

One day, I learned that a famous performer was

going to give a performance at the palace. Young girls, however, were not allowed at banquets. Brunhilde convinced the "very well-behaved Clothilde" to ignore the social conventions. We hid behind some curtains. My dog, Brux, who followed me everywhere, almost gave us away. In that uncomfortable position, in the midst of all the commotion, we heard in bits and pieces the *Niebelungen*, our national epic poem. We were struggling against fatigue and sleepiness. I lifted a corner of the curtain, and there was my uncle Gondebaud, seated directly in front of us. He said nothing, but I definitely saw him give me a quick wink.

At the end, I heard the victory of Atilla lamented, he who had driven my ancestors from their country. I wondered where we could be better off than here in our Sapaudia. I could not regret those cold lands from which we came, but I kept from saying so.

Around the age of fifteen, I was given permission to attend the intimate dinners where my parents entertained only a few, select guests. At these, poems were recited, music was played, and above all, there was conversation of good company. At these dinners, I would meet the elite of Gaul. I remember Sidonius, the bishop of Clermont, and I was dazzled by his mind. My mother cited his charity as exemplary. He even went so far as to give his silver dinnerware to the poor. His people complained to us about it one day! And yet I held something against Sidonius. He had made fun of our soldiers, calling them barbarians who smelled of garlic and rancid butter! My mother said, "He is a great lord, and he is pained at having to be subject to us."

"No doubt", I retorted, "but whose fault is that? All the Roman elite had to do was to defend themselves better. Instead, they had become soft from luxury, had given up having children, and had entrusted themselves to mercenary soldiers. Had God perhaps punished them? In any case", I concluded, "we bear primary responsibility for what happens to us." To which my mother's conclusion was "In that case, consider well what *you* do, and look at the consequences of it as best you can."

Interrupting my daydreaming, a servant woman suddenly enters. She exclaims that the physicians have forbidden me to get up early. So here I am back in bed, awaiting my daughter-in-law, Radegonde, who at the moment is staying close by me. My son Clothaire has granted me this favor, and Radegonde is happy to be away from the corruption of her husband's court. Here, she lives according to her heart, hiding her radiant beauty behind dark veils, she washes the feet of pilgrims and cares for the sick who hurry to the tomb of Saint Martin, hoping for a miracle. Behind the most repulsive of faces, she sees only the image of the suffering Christ. To everyone she gives her glowing smile and her comforting words. I love her and admire her. The difference in our ages in no way interferes with the communion of our souls.

I hear her footsteps on the staircase. We are to go together to our Lord's Supper. Blessed be God who, in this way, has given me, on the verge of death, the grace of a last friendship.

II

Today I am crippled with pain. Humidity comes up from the river and penetrates my bones. Seated next to the brazier and wrapped warmly in a hooded cape, I listen to the sound of the waters swollen by the long, hard winter.

In Geneva, we lived near the lake, and I used to fall asleep listening to the splashing of the waves. Half asleep, I thought I could hear my father's dear voice; I hoped to dream about him so as to see him again.

He had died suddenly. The other sufferings of my life have not made me forget that terrible moment. I was spinning yarn in my mother's chamber, chatting with the servants, when people came running into the antechamber. Shouts rang out. They informed me that I was fatherless!

For a long time, Mama kept turning her regrets over and over in her mind; she should have been more forceful in urging her husband to listen to the doctors. He scorned their advice. According to him, there was no better medicine than a glass of that good wine produced from the neighboring vineyards. His complexion was the color of brick; he puffed whenever he trained with his equerry.

My uncles divided their brother's kingdom among themselves. They let us choose between living in Vienne with Gondebaud or in Geneva with Godegisile. While we preferred the more cheerful Gondebaud, we chose the other uncle because he was going to become a Catholic.

In Geneva, we led a secluded life. My mother, my sister, and I devoted ourselves to prayer and works of charity. The poor came to our door one after another, where the doorman had orders to welcome them always. My mother became famous there, too, for her charity. Though it has been some thirty years since she died, she is remembered still.

Sédéleube soon left us for the cloister. I remained behind to keep my mother company, but I had made up my mind to join my sister as soon as possible. The sudden death of our father had made me aware of the fragility of human life. I liked to quote the psalmist, "As for man, his days are like the grass." From many of our former courtiers, I had met with both indifference and neglect. I used to flee from people in order to take refuge in Christ. He was my favorite friend; I knew I could trust him. I prayed a great deal, particularly for the conversion of my people. I had the joy of seeing this come to pass. The Burgundians are now Catholics. The Lord said, "In its time I will hasten it."

Prudentius used to write to us often, as did Avitus,

the noble bishop of Vienne. In our adversity, he was our friend and most devoted advisor.

Our house in Geneva was not large, but it was pleasant. It looked out over gardens that sloped gently down to the water's edge. In the summertime, we used to spend a great deal of time in a pavilion surrounded by flowers. There, we enjoyed the most beautiful spectacle that Gaul could offer. Tall mountains, sometimes still covered in snow, were reflected in the lake. I loved the mountains just as I loved the water that flowed down from them. Before so much splendor, I would praise the Lord, "How great and beautiful are your works."

Then one day, my life changed dramatically. It was on a gray morning in the beginning of winter. I was reading to my mother from the Bible. The gentle household sounds surrounded us like a reassuring cocoon. Braziers and curtains protected us from the already biting cold. I heard whispering in the vestibule where straw had been spread to muffle the sound of footsteps. Then, the butler raised the door curtain, and Godegisile entered the room accompanied by a shaft of cold air. We were surprised because his visits were infrequent. I had barely time to stand up when he had already made his greeting and an armchair had been brought forward for him.

With the usual formalities quickly observed, he informed us that a message from Gondebaud had arrived and that it concerned us.

I believe I can still hear our astonished silence and the

monotonous sound of the water-clock loudly marking the minutes. Then the stupefying words fell: Clovis, the young king of the Salien Franks, the new master of northern Gaul, was asking for Princess Clothilde's hand in marriage.

Godegisile was obviously pleased, and he urged me to accept as soon as possible. Those Franks are somewhat boorish, he admitted, but the prospective husband was of noble birth and I could not hope for a better match. But Gondebaud, perhaps less enthusiastic, insisted that I be allowed some time for reflection.

My first impulse was to refuse. After all, Clovis was pagan. Was that not worse than Arianism? Carétène, although hesitant, maintained that a pagan was easier to convert. But from where does Clovis know me? My mother reminded me of a banquet we had attended the previous summer. There were very few guests. I had noticed a group of foreigners to whom our sovereigns showed great courtesy. From their shaved necks and their glowing red clothing, I had recognized them as Franks. But I had paid less attention to them than to the music, whose soft harmonies, in keeping with the colors of the setting sun above the lake, crowned my happiness.

Those Franks had said flattering things about me to their chief. They found me elegant and modest. Clovis had been charmed by this to the point of wanting to marry me. At least that is what was being said! But I sensed other motives behind this request for marriage. Clovis must have coveted an alliance with the Burgundians. He had his reasons at which I did not take offense. But my own reasoning forbade me to marry a pagan.

Then I was surprised to see Bishop Avitus arrive. He had braved the dangerous wintry roads to be with me as the exponent of the Catholic point of view. Have no doubt, he told me, that God was giving me a great mission: the conversion of Clovis, who, the bishop sensed, would be the "arbiter of his time". The example set by the king would be decisive. Heresy must not win over the Frankish people, who seemed destined for great things. Now two of Clovis' sisters had just converted to Arianism. Perhaps the fate of the Church and of Gaul was depending on me.

Suddenly I saw myself again in the palace garden in Lyon. I remembered the words of Bishop Prudentius about the fate of important people in the world. Then I realized that the time had come for me to accept the mission that God was bestowing on me through the mediation of his bishop. Avitus promised me the support of the entire clergy and the prayers of all the people. I handed myself over to the will of the Lord, for it was not due to ambition or to any other motive that I was accepting this marriage, but rather for the glory of God and the well-being of his Church.

As soon as my acceptance became known, I was swept into a whirlwind. My uncle Godegisile was insistent on having us move into the palace with him. I think it was more to keep an eye on me than to honor me. I suspected that he wanted to prevent contact between Gondebaud and me without his knowledge. The division of my father's kingdom had set the two brothers at odds. Alas, later events confirmed the estrangement of which I had a foreboding.

The hasty preparation of my trousseau distracted my mother from her sadness. Tailors, shoemakers, and jewelers worked unceasingly on my behalf. Syrian and Jewish merchants presented their silks and perfumes, and maidservants filled enormous chests that had triple locks. Afterward, all these people would follow me everywhere, and goodness only knows how much running about I did.

I also went to see my sister, Sédéleube, as often as possible at the Abbey of Saint Victor. On the day of my departure, she gave me a small reliquary from which I was never after separated. We were not able to hold back our tears, for we sensed that we would never see each other again on this earth.

During this time, I had become engaged by proxy. A Burgundian delegation met with Clovis' ambassadors at Chalon. According to ancient custom, I was symbolically bought for a gold sou and a silver denarius.

With the spring came the time to depart. I bade farewell to all that I loved, and in my mother's arms, I poured out the last tears that I was ever to shed publicly. From then on, in all circumstances, I would conduct myself as royal dignity required.

A numerous party accompanied me, and my dear Brunhilde was part of it. I was later to have her married to a noble Frank. She died in childbirth, as did too many of our young women. Heaven had not provided her with a robust constitution like my own. Before I reached this advanced age, I did not know illness. In fact, I followed Clovis almost everywhere, braving bad weather and enduring discomfort. I was his wife; I also wanted to be his inseparable friend and companion.

It was my uncle Gondebaud who escorted me to the border. I could guess his ulterior motives: he feared Clovis' ambition. He wanted to be assured of my goodwill. But I remained silent about anything that concerned my future. I knew that from then on it was Clovis, and none other, who would decide my future. Yet as long as my husband lived, I succeeded in avoiding the serious disputes between the Franks and the Burgundians. My sons, alas, did not follow suit.

When the heavy mule-drawn litter started out on the stone-paved road, I was very right to recall my mission in order not to look back with sadness. But I let myself be distracted by the voyage. We made use of the old network of Roman roads that were still in good condition. Since Gondebaud had planned for fresh horses and since we were exempt from stops at tollgates because of our social rank, we advanced as fast as road conditions permitted. My uncle did not always choose the shortest route. Desirous of taking maximum advantage of these days stolen from the concerns that come with power, he decided to make some detours that inevitably led us to places that we enjoyed greatly. One day, along the River Saône, we went through a wet plain where the chariots almost sank into the ground. But vineyards stretched out on the hillsides that my uncle said were the true gems of his kingdom. We went down into cellars where precious harvests were stored. Gondebaud claimed that aging in barrels gave those wines a flavor superior to those kept in clay jars . . . The famous Burgundy wine!

I loved the company of my uncle. That jovial man was very cultured. He read the Greek authors and was fascinated by legal issues. He had a code drawn up that the people refer to as the Gombette Law. Clovis was then to draw inspiration from it for his Salic Law. But Gondebaud could also prove to be fearsome. He carried cruelty to the point of murdering his own brother. But I prefer to chase away the frightful memory of Godegisile's massacre and keep in my memory the redheaded giant who would hide a doll behind his back, or the lovable voyage companion who would converse enough for two people and drink accordingly.

While still in Burgundy, we came across numerous fortified towns. Country villas whose well-cultivated fields we admired were not rare, and Gondebaud knew their proprietors, almost all of whom were Burgundians. Upon their arrival, our ancestors had obtained grants for the richest lands from the hard-pressed Roman governors. Some properties had been abandoned due to war, but more often they were grabbed from their lawful owners. So the Romans thought of the Burgundians as thieves! The Franks were fortunate in not having to drive anyone away. They occupied regions that had been devastated and in part returned to wasteland. Thus they were able to appear more as protectors than as invaders.

We finally arrived at the border. It was pouring rain. Water was streaming over the shimmering clothing worn by Frankish noblemen walking toward us. My uncle, draped in his purple cloak as the "master of the militia", watched them come. Everything in his bearing showed well the honor he was paying to the king of the Franks by having agreed to this alliance with his niece.

My sadness returned when I saw Gondebaud's silhouette disappearing into the fog. We then set out again on the road with new leading escorts. The sight of the Frankish kingdom was not conducive to dispelling melancholy. By roads difficult to maneuver, we proceeded through thick forests. Here, there were few human traces except for some colliers' huts in clearings or a swineherd, well-protected by his thick cloak and hood, leading his dark herd in an oak grove. We dozed in our carts, the horsemen exchanging short calls and our horses quivering at the howling of wolves.

We were nearing Villery. At the edge of a village, we saw a horseman sheltering under a thatch roof. He advised us that Clovis was nearby. My heart was beating fast. My future—and much more than that—depended on this meeting.

I instructed my ladies to dress me. I was not a coquette, but I wanted to honor my fiancé. In spite of Brunhilde, who found the color not very flattering for a blond, I put on a white dress embroidered with gold.

I had chosen the color that symbolizes purity. I was offering Clovis a heart and body never before given away.

A bronze mirror and an ivory comb were taken from a small casket. I was adorned with jewels of brilliant colors: a necklace woven of gold thread, a chain with flowers with garnet centers, heavy silver bracelets encrusted with gold and amethysts, earrings made of filigree and pearl. I rejected perfumes that were too musky, but I did agree to have my friend decorate my hair with ribbons of red and green, colors dear to the Franks. I was just barely ready when the procession came to a sudden stop. Horses neighed, and I pulled aside the litter's curtain and saw a group of horsemen galloping toward us. One of them had hair flowing down to his shoulders. It was Clovis! Frankish rulers never cut their hair, a sign of royal power.

Barely had I time to see him, and he was already there. He jumped down from his horse and came forward in a rapid stride. He did not allow me time to descend and greet him with the fine words of welcome I had long since prepared. He took me in his arms amid cheering and proclaimed his joy in meeting me at last. His joy, as I found out later, was genuine. The sight of me had reassured him: in this fiancée in the immaculate dress, he had chosen well. Thanks be to God, he never changed his mind. As for me, at that moment, I placed my trust in him. He never betrayed it.

BRUNOR

Clovis was then twenty-five. Having become king at fifteen, he had right away earned his reputation as "illustrious in combat". His people believed him to be descended from the gods. His warriors idolized a chief who was always victorious and who showered them with booty. I watched this horseman with the face framed in a halo of blond hair who rode alongside my carriage door, slender, with a keen face, short of word, and quick of gesture. I sensed that Avitus had not been mistaken: God had destined Clovis for great things.

At Troyes, accommodations had been prepared for us at the bishop's palace. The rain had ceased, and the air was becoming spring-like. I felt happy. While secluded in my room, I was suddenly aware that at no time since our meeting had I remembered that Clovis was pagan. The presence of my fiancé had erased my anxiety. Then I turned toward the image of Christ that had been placed by my bedside. I prayed to him fervently. I was no longer asking for the conversion of the king of the Franks; I was asking for the conversion of a man I already loved and from whom I wished nothing to separate me from that time on.

III

When our merry procession left Troyes, the weather was beautiful. And even the countryside was smiling more. I rode horseback next to my fiancé, secretly observing him. I noticed that his face would light up only for me. The escort eagerly obeyed its master. At that time I recalled an anecdote that had been recounted as far away as the court in Geneva.

The city of Soissons had been taken and pillaged by the Franks. Its bishop had sent to ask Clovis the favor of having a precious vessel returned to him. Clovis asked his soldiers to grant him this object. All agreed except one, who was so insolent as to strike the vessel with his battle-axe. The king did not say a word. He was able to wait months for his vengeance. The occasion presented itself at the time of a military review on the Field of Mars. Clovis approached the recalcitrant soldier and criticized the poor condition of his weapons, which Clovis threw to the ground. When the man reached down to pick them up, the king smashed his head. There was no more dissent after that! The Frankish army became an obedient instrument at the service of the ambitions of its leader.

I sensed in my fiancé one of those personalities that is not satisfied with a few successes. Master of the northern part of Gaul, Clovis was now looking beyond that. In a country shaken by invasions, contested by several rulers, and, for all intents and purposes, abandoned by the far-off emperor, the Frankish king had understood that everything was possible for whoever would take it by force or by cunning. He lacked neither the one nor the other. But he did not have the help of the Lord. I was going to dedicate myself to providing him with that.

Toward evening, we neared Soissons. Upon seeing its walls, Clovis displayed one of his rare smiles. It was his capital. He had conquered it recently. For it, he had forsaken Tournai, his family home. Later he would also leave Soissons, but not without regret. It has remained dear to me also as there are so many happy memories attached to it.

We soon heard the sound of trumpets announcing the arrival of our procession. Triumphal arches made of branches had been erected at the city gate. Two tall figures in white stood out from the crowd: they were Principius, bishop of Soissons, and his brother, Remigius, bishop of Reims. In the commotion of our arrival, we exchanged few words. But I suspected that these men had played their part in the holy conspiracy that had ended in my marriage. The same secret mission was leading us: to convert a soul who first had to be convinced.

I awoke early on the morning of my wedding. The dawn was gray. Rain was beating against the window-panes. Servants entered carrying a large vat. Armed with pitchers and soap, the maids busied themselves with my bathing and dressing. New faces mingled with the familiar ones. I welcomed these Frankish servants. I had decided to let nothing show of my closer attachment to those who had accompanied me to my new life.

The chambermaids clothed me in a dress of violet-colored silk and then in a red tunic embroidered with gold. Over that they adorned me with masses of jewels dominated by gold, garnets, and amethysts. Red-silk ribbons were entwined with my loosened hair.

Looking like a reliquary, I went out to meet my husband. He, too, was resplendent. He had worn the purple cloak of Roman generals. The emperor had given Clovis this honorary title. A heavy gold bracelet, emblem of Frankish royalty, shone on his wrist.

I believe we made a magnificent couple. Our subjects cheered us when we appeared at the doors of the alabaster palace. The leuds, noble companions of the king, brandished their weapons in our honor and called on their warrior gods. Among the elite guard, the "truste", I recognized the men who had been at the banquet in Geneva, and also those who had escorted me to Villery. I noticed in the crowd some clothing in the Roman style. Clovis had brought into his inner circle some old inhabitants of the land. My father and uncles had done the same. I approved of this attitude. In any case we had need of them in order to carry out the task of governing.

But my husband was looking beyond immediate concerns. He sought to become, one day, the ruler of a people who were not divided between victors and vanquished.

The banquet seemed long to me. We presided, seated on our bronze thrones. The long tables, draped in linen, were decorated with garlands where the bright green of ivy was coupled with the dark green of laurel. Greenery was also strewn on the marble floor.

There was an abundance of food, but less varied and delicate than at my home. In accordance with Frankish custom, the soup was served first. Then huge, silver, game-laden platters were brought around, accompanied by very spicy sauces. There were few vegetables in this feast. But the desserts, creams, candied fruits, and dried fruits, were served in elegant dishes made of polished wood or ceramic. Every guest had pyramids of wheat bread nearby.

Swarms of servers were constantly rushing from the kitchen. Lined up behind the guests, cup-bearers were quick to serve them something to drink. Beer and wines from Italy, the East, and Gaul streamed into the gold and silver goblets.

Singers and musicians tried to hold their own above the growing uproar. And a short silence greeted the entrance of acrobats or dancing girls. My subjects' manners seemed coarse to me, for the tablecloths were quickly soiled, bones littered the floor, and voices became hoarse.

Suddenly I felt overcome with sadness that was unaccustomed, for I was not in the habit of feeling sorry for myself. But I let myself be carried away by it, tempted, no doubt, by the demon whose plans I would be thwarting. The enemy took advantage of it and made himself the master of my imagination. I saw before me only strange faces—beginning with that of my husband, the implacable chief of these cold and violent men. How many intrigues was I going to have to face? Would I be sufficiently on my guard? Would I be able to make myself valued enough to triumph over the pagan party at court? Through smoke from the torches, I searched in vain for my own countrymen. I felt completely alone. I forgot my heavenly allies and my earthly ones, including the powerful network of support led by the great Remigius.

I envied my sister's life in her peaceful convent, occupied with her prayers, reading, and the care of the medicinal plants in her little garden. The temptation to doubt and discouragement was carrying me away. I was drawn out of it by Clovis, who, apparently, had been wholly occupied with his guests until that moment. He brought me back to reality and to himself by placing his hand on mine. On my finger, he slipped a ring adorned with a marvelous sapphire. He thus knew my taste for that stone and for that color. "I chose it",

BRUNOR

he told me, "because of its similarity to your eyes." That gesture and those words gave me confidence and joy. Never since have I been separated from this ring. I want it to accompany me in my tomb.

We arose at last and left the hall amid the cheering of guests, who were on the verge of intoxication. It was Godfried, a noble Burgundian representing my family, who picked me up and carried me over the threshold of my nuptial chamber. A soft light fell from the bronze candelabras. The maids had used a heating pan to warm the bed draped in linen and in purple covers. While they busied themselves with my nighttime preparations, I gathered my thoughts in prayer, begging God to bless Clovis and me.

In the morning, my husband offered me, as a traditional present, several towns from which, from then on, I was to draw my income. I thanked him with a kiss. Between us, there would never be a need for many words.

A servant woman suddenly interrupts my reverie. "Venerable queen, here is your Easter meal. It is larger than usual. You have eggs, lentils, and even some cream, the cream to which the nuns are so partial."

I thank her with a smile, and I remind her that she must set up the chess set because the chaplain will be coming for a game with me. These meetings serve as a pretext for serious conversation. The future of the church is what concerns us. Formerly, if it was enough to increase the number of places of worship, Clovis took care of it, now, together with my sons, I continue that work. But for many, Christianity too often amounts to superficial practices. So much paganism remains, especially in the countryside. Even the word "peasant" is on the way to becoming synonymous with "pagan". I used to know villages where they worshiped upright stones. I have seen processions honoring a horned statue, a veritable image of the devil! Even in the city and here close by me, who does not harbor his little superstitions?

"I still remember your anger when you learned that many artisans would not work on Thursdays", said the chaplain, moving a pawn.

"Yes, I summoned the master craftsmen. They denied wanting to honor the the feast day of Jupiter in that way."

"They were alleging traditions and customs."

"I made them understand that it was time to change these things and that I would not tolerate such behavior any longer in Saint Martin's city."

"You know, they were telling the truth. These pagan remembrances are like empty shells. It's enough to baptize them."

"Yes, let's place crosses on the upright stones and statues of saints at the sacred springs."

"Above all, without violence and with great patience!"

"Above all, my father, let us pray to the many saints

who protect this country. For great is the task that God has set for us."

I look distractedly at the chessboard, and my thoughts drift far away from it. I imagine a different chessboard, a universal one, whose limits I do not know. On it a decisive game is being played, for there, Good is confronting Evil.

May God grant that, in this combat, my people, in the service of Good, may spread the faith among the most distant of nations.

IV

Of my first year of marriage, I have nothing but happy memories.

I was overwhelmed with things to do. Escorted by the majordomo, I would go everywhere in the palace of which I was from then on mistress. In my presence, the servants would open the massive locks of the heavy coffers. I would inventory their contents and insert new herbal sachets as a precaution against insects. I changed the decoration of the staterooms. I would go down as far as the kitchens, where, in front of the huge fireplaces, the cooks, shirtless, would be skimming foam from huge cauldrons and turning spits on which morsels of game were skewered. The ceiling was invisible because of all the hams and sausages hanging from it. The inhabitants of this country made them better than anyone. Hoards of wine casks were lined up in the cellar. Clovis liked nothing better than soup and spit-roasted pork basted with beer. But he had to offer his guests plenty of wine and and costly dishes.

That spring, Clovis did not undertake any military expeditions, so we spent a great deal of time together.

I even went hunting with him, despite my lack of attraction to this sport that Franks love almost as much as warfare. Dressed in short clothing in the Frankish style, I would urge my horse forward behind the pack of wolf dogs and mastiffs, pleased at being a good horsewoman.

Such an exercise could be dangerous. The hunters would encounter deer but also wild boar, wolves, and at times bison and aurochs. They preferred the spear and the cutlass to the bow and arrow. One of our party perished in one of these body-to-body struggles. His corpse was brought back in the soft light of torches held aloft by slaves. Throughout the night, the wailing of mourners could be heard. The deceased was of high rank. I was present at his funeral. Dressed in his finest clothing and adorned with jewels, he was laid out on a carpet at the bottom of a grave. Near him were placed his weapons, his longbow made of yewwood, and some jars containing food and drink. Then three arrows were ceremoniously shot aloft. The deceased's favorite horse, harnessed with his finest ornamental gear, was then brought forth, was sacrificed, and was buried with his master.

I heard it lamented that this man had not died in battle, otherwise he would have gone directly to Valhallah. I said a silent prayer for this soul who did not know the true God.

"How can they make the other world a slavish copy of our own?", I asked Clovis. I would seize every opportunity to emphasize the absurdity of the pagan customs. Sometimes I even dared to suggest that my husband was paying empty worship to nonexistent gods from whom he could expect no help at all. My own God, with one word, had created heaven and earth.

Clovis would be evasive. One day when I was a little too insistent, he reminded me that he was descended from a god, which justified his power and the nobility of his bloodline. In any case, he reckoned that only warrior gods suited a warrior people.

My husband's family welcomed me with kindness. I formed a special friendship with my sister-in-law, Lantilde, and I was affectionate toward Thierry, Clovis' son from a previous union with a princess from the banks of the Rhine. The child became attached to me and actually brought me more contentment than did those of my own blood. He would accompany me on my walks around Soissons, proudly taking on the role of chief escort.

War had left its mark everywhere. Even in these rich lands, fields remained fallow and villages seemed abandoned. The Franks were numerous in this region. From far off I would recognize their longhouses made of wood or of cob, with roofs of reed and thatch. On occasion, I used to dismount and cross over the protective fence. I would get bogged down in the mud. The poultry would flee, shrieking, and pigs would grunt in their wallows. A cow might stick its head out of the door of the shack. The dogs would bark furiously and pull on their spiked collars. Most often the men would be away. The women would approach timidly, preceded by blond children whose clear eyes shone brightly in their dirty faces. Once reassured, the women would invite us to enter their huts. The smell of smoke was suffocating. In the half-dark, I could pick out, little by little, some straw mattresses, a chest, some skins hanging on the walls, and several earthenware utensils.

Most often, young Thierry would remain in the doorway, visibly unhappy. One day, he reproached me for those malodorous visits: "What interest can you possibly have in these peasants?"

"You know", I answered, "the powerful have a duty toward the humble. It's Christ's message."

"Only force counts in this world", he answered.

Such remarks made the need to bring the Gospel to this harsh place more urgent for me.

Summer came. We left Soissons and the stench of its muddy alleys. Beyond the city walls, the countryside smelled of freshly cut hay. A throng of wagons loaded with furniture jolted along the Roman roadway toward the villa in Juvigny. We were to spend the summer there, living off the resources of the land. Like all Franks, Clovis liked the nomadic life, so we often changed residence.

The royal residence disappointed me. There was no comparison with that of my parents, even less so with the sumptuous houses of the former nobles of this country. Here, plain buildings, sometimes of wood, were arranged around a flagstone courtyard. A large pond was used for thermal baths. Water came to us from a well in the backyard. The peaceful sound of the creaking of its pulley and impact of the buckets against the edge accompanied our days.

The villa offered everything needed to support a sizeable household: a bread oven, a dairy, a forge, a woodworking shop, and even a women's hall where workers wove wool, hemp, and linen. Wheat was grown on the surrounding plateaus. Fruit trees grew on the hillsides, and beehives provided a delicious honey. I used to gather armfuls of flowers, whose perfume filled the house.

Then the smell of burning dead leaves replaced that of newly cut grass. Summer was coming gently to an end. One afternoon, as I remember, I was lying in my bedchamber. A breeze, as yet warm, was moving the curtain. Turtledoves were cooing, and beneath my window, little boys were playing jacks. Then it was that I first felt the child I was expecting move inside me. To be bringing forth life filled me with joy.

I remember, too, a neighborly visit from Remigius. In his honor, I decorated the table with the petals from the last of our roses. But at the meal, he paid only a polite attention. He was hiding his concern about something else. "Your lordship", he finally said to Clovis, "I wonder just how far the persecution by the Visigoths will go. Are you aware that they are seizing bishops? They have even imprisoned some." Then, filled with indignation, he became silent. I was about to intervene when the bishop exclaimed, "What will they gain by making themselves detested by their subjects? If only they would take as their example your own behavior, noble king." He then held out his hands toward us and said fervently, "Venerable sovereigns, God blesses you for the attention you pay to the bishops' advice. Your people are benefiting from it. The only remaining hope of the episcopacy of Gaul is in you."

Clovis lowered his head. When he raised it again, he looked very intently at Remigius, and I thought he was on the verge of speaking. But he stood up, apologized, said goodbye, and left.

I hurried to reassure Remigius: "The king understood your message. You know how much he admires you. He revealed his feelings by departing."

"How does he listen to you when you talk to him of what is so important to us?" the bishop asked.

"He is favorably disposed, but I am careful not to harass him."

"That seems wise to me. It is necessary that you first gain your husband's respect and trust. By showing your love for your husband, you will bring him to the God of love."

"Should I say something about his own interests? Show him that Gaul is his if he makes the wise choice and becomes the only Catholic ruler?"

"Why not? Your husband is not a private individual. All his decisions have political effects. But first of all, Clovis will convert because we will have prayed a great deal."

Our guest left, and I sat for a moment on the steps. It was a fine evening. A child was throwing stones into the pond. Rings of water radiated out from the point of impact, growing larger little by little up to the water's edge. Thus, thought I, do my words spread, little by little, in the mind of Clovis. And one day, the truth will catch hold of him.

With the arrival of winter, we returned to the alabaster palace. Clovis was away more often. In secret meetings with his men, where many jugs of barley beer were emptied, he was preparing for his spring campaign. Messages were going out to other rulers—even to the emperor in Constantinople. One of these ambassadors described for me that city with its golden palace, sumptuous ceremonies, and dignitaries resplendent in precious stones. It was truly the capital city of the world!

Once, when I was marveling, in the presence of Clovis, at the prestige of the emperor, he said to me coldly, "Too far away for people here to fear him, but still powerful enough for them to draw some benefit from it."

"The emperor is Catholic", I reminded him. "He will certainly take as his close ally a ruler of the same religion."

"Above all, the emperor will see where his interest lies, and I will see where my own lies", Clovis concluded dryly.

This dryness, unusual with respect to me, did not offend me. I preferred it to evasive answers. Perhaps the king was finally facing the idea of his conversion.

BRUNOR

He was living through a difficult transition. The moment was filled with uncertainty. It was necessary that I be more present and more discreet than ever.

I received some reassurance at that time: Geneviève, the best-known woman in Gaul, wrote to me from Paris. Her fame extended even as far as the East. From her childhood, she had dedicated herself to God. She had founded a community devoted to prayer, poverty, and charity. In return, God showered her with gifts. She performed miracles. My parents admired her; Clovis venerated her. The Parisians loved her as a mother. She had saved their city by sustaining their courage against the invaders. She was in fact part of the "holy conspiracy" to convert the Franks, so I owed my marriage to her as well.

I took up her letter with respect. The venerable lady saw in my marriage Providence at work. She encouraged me and assured me of her support. I very much wanted to meet her. And she must also have wanted to know me because she was willing to travel, even at her great age, in order to do so. I can see her now, stepping from her palanquin. I rushed forward to her majestic figure draped in white. I anticipated her own greeting by kissing her hand. Then she held me against her heart. I shall never forget the extraordinarily kind consideration she showed everyone. She was one of those pure hearts who see God and spread peace. I would have wanted to meet her more often: I would have become a better person. I placed myself in the care of her prayers. And now that she is in eternity, I pray to her.

Through my efforts, Geneviève is now buried in the basilica that overlooks Lutetia. Clovis wanted to lie near her. And there also is where I had the coffins of my daughter and grandson placed. I hope to join them soon. Near them, under the protection of the Parisians, I will await the resurrection.

V

Our bishop, Injuriosus, enjoys visiting me. We speak with each other about the problems of the Church. But today, taking advantage of a ray of sunshine, we go downstairs to the garden. I want him to admire my flowers. We walk through solid masses of them toward the river, where sailboats are rushing off toward Marmoutiers. I watch their progress for a moment; I enjoyed so much going on pilgrimage to the hermitages of Martin's first companions.

The chief gardener comes up to us timidly. Clovis brought him back among the prisoners from his expedition to Armorique. I freed him, as recommended by the Church. He is very devoted to me. I notice that in the crook of his arm, he is carrying some sort of bundle wrapped in rags. Suddenly I see that it is a baby. His most recent, he tells me. I know that all the others died in infancy. And now this one, in turn, is ill. The father begs me to help the baby, to send my physician to him. I promise to do so at once. The man drops to his knees and hands me the poor creature. From that colorless little face, two immense, sad eyes look solemnly at me. I become unsteady, and the bishop grasps my arm.

"Are you feeling ill? Do you want me to take you back?"

"No, it is just a painful memory. I suddenly saw again the face of Ingomer . . . yes, my first child . . . the son so eagerly awaited. I was taking him out of his little cradle and placing him in his little coffin . . ."

"I know that you had had him baptized."

"Yes, Clovis had agreed to it. I wanted to impress him with a sumptuous ceremony: the church disappeared beneath all the purple and oriental rugs. Alas! Barely had he been baptized when our son fell ill. The medicines were ineffective. Then I permitted an amulet to be hung about the baby's neck. Some servants made strange incantations over his cradle."

"Nevertheless, you had prayers said for the child?"

"Yes, in all the churches in Soissons. But one morning, Ingomer died. When I was sleeping from exhaustion, I had a dream: I was walking in the garden in Geneva in the rain . . . I awoke: Brunhilde was bent over me crying. But I did not cry! I was filled with rebellion! Why had God let my son die in his white baptismal robe? Was he not worthy of special protection?"

"And the king?"

"The king? His attitude added to my suffering. He avoided me. But when he did come, it was in order to say bitter things to me: 'It is your God who caused the death of our child. If I had consecrated him to mine, he would still be alive . . .' Then my bitterness suddenly died down. I turned to God in a surge of confidence. These words of faith came to my lips: 'I thank God, who has deigned to welcome my son into his kingdom. In that way, he is sparing him suffering on earth.' God had inspired me, and at the same time he touched Clovis' heart. The king took my hand in his, and we remained silent. But that silence no longer had any hostility in it. With my head on my husband's shoulder, I was finally able to cry. Later, I even dared to say, 'I want another baby!' and dared to add, 'I beg you to permit him to be baptized'. 'So be it', the king responded, 'but pray to your God, because I will not willingly sacrifice another child to him!'

"When I found myself pregnant again, I repeated this prayer, 'Lord, please let this child live! Do so for your glory!'

"Clodomir was baptized at birth. Then right away illness seized him. I was reliving a nightmare. Clovis reproached me. He again regretted not having consecrated the infant to his gods. But I rejected sorcerers, sorceresses, and amulets. On the cradle, we placed a piece of blessed Martin's tunic. Clodomir was cured. In his joy, Clovis ordered the freeing of numerous prisoners, and he lifted recently imposed fines. But his joy did not compare with mine. I promised Martin that I would make a pilgrimage to Tours, and I showered alms on a crowd of poor people."

"Clovis was on the path to conversion", said Injuriosus.

"Yes, Remigius glimpsed the fruit of ten years of effort. Even more than ten years. I found the letter that he had sent to Clovis when he was raised on the shield as the new king. In the letter, he asked Clovis to make sure that the Lord does not turn his back on him. He strongly suggested that Clovis take advice from his bishops for the good of the land entrusted to his authority."

"That is in fact what the young king did!"

"Yes, and Remigius was the principal bishop in his government. Clovis held him in high regard."

"The king had understood where his interest lay. His conversion would gain him the support of the people of Gaul and of the powerful bishops."

"Indeed! But in becoming a Christian he would be losing the prestige of having descended from gods. And how would a warrior people accept a peaceable God? On the other hand, what if Clothilde, Remigius and Geneviève were right; what if there were only one all-powerful God?

"I observed my husband's hesitations. And I understood them. It was such a major step to take. I respected Clovis too much to think that he would accept conversion out of calculated self-interest. I prayed unceasingly for the king.

"Then God interceded. That spring, danger was reported at the river Rhine. The Rhenish Franks had just been attacked by the Alamanni. With the end of the river floods came the military surge against our kingdom.

"Clovis and the army left in haste. But this campaign was not like the others. One day a messenger arrived back unexpectedly. He told of a terrible defeat. The Alamanni had slaughtered a great number of Franks, and nothing was known about Clovis. We were all left horror-stricken when we heard a horse at full gallop; a royal guardsman was trying hard to catch up with the bearer of bad news. A complete reversal of fortune had taken place. There had been a miracle, which the guardsman himself had witnessed. He happened to be very near the king. At the height of battle, encircled and desperate, Clovis had suddenly lifted his hands heavenward, shouting out, 'God of Clothilde, if you give me this victory, I will have myself baptized!'

"Everything then was completely reversed. Our warriors had taken heart. The king of the Alamanni was dead. This defeat was transformed into a brilliant victory."

"The king called on Clothilde's God", murmured Injuriosus.

"Yes, that is what touched me most in the report."

"I can imagine with what impatience you waited for the vanquisher's return."

"I counted the days up to the first of April. Then at last I was able to hold him in my arms. He spoke right away about baptism. Always impatient, he wanted to know as soon as possible this God who had answered him."

"I have heard it said that he was present at a number of miracles while on the way back."

"In Toul, he had met Vedastus, a holy man with whom he shared the road for a while. Clovis witnessed a number of cures. Above all, that of a blind man made an impression on him; it was a beggar whose eyelids were stuck shut. 'In the name of Jesus Christ, may your eyes be opened', Vedastus had cried. And the man stood up with open eyes, fixing his new gaze upon my husband."

"Certainly God wanted this in order to strengthen the newborn faith of the king."

"My husband has always been responsive to wonders . . . As to the baptism, I notified Remigius right away. In spite of his advanced age, he hurried over alone, at night and on horseback. We resolved to keep the royal decision secret. It was agreed that the bishop would discreetly instruct his illustrious catechumen. Various pretexts were found for the meetings. Remigius told me how pleased he was that Clovis was ardently taking up the study of the Holy Scriptures. I gave my husband a book of the Gospels, illuminated and set with beautiful stones. I was there the day Remigius recounted the Passion of Christ. You can guess with what eloquence! The king then cried out, 'If only I had been there with my Frankish men . . .' "

"Clovis was a true soldier of Christ."

"Even so, the king remained careful. He could not put off for long the announcement of his conversion. His baptism was not the act of a private individual; it would involve the entire people. But how would the Franks receive his decision?

"To his surprise, when he spoke to the nobles,

he found few reservations. Many among them even wanted to be baptized with him. The prayers that had surrounded us had borne fruit."

"Like everyone, I have heard much talk about this baptism. But I have never had an account from your own lips."

"There is nothing I like recalling more. That event was the summit of my life! . . .

"It was Christmas! Reims was resplendent. In the sweet-smelling torchlight, houses disappeared beneath embroidered wall hangings and costly rugs. A huge crowd was packed within the walls of the city. At the palace, there was a parade of important, influential persons. Bishops arrived from all over Gaul. The baptism of the king of the Franks was delighting the entire Catholic country. Unfortunately, Avitus had been kept back at Vienne. But just at the moment that our procession was starting out, we were handed a letter from him: "Your faith is our victory!" he wrote. Just a few words had said it all.

"The night before the ceremony, Clovis and I had prayed in the church crypt where Remigius liked to meditate. It seemed that we could feel the mysterious presence of all our holy protectors gathered around us in the half-light of flickering candles. With what joy and faith I invoked them. Time seemed short to me. I had no sense of fatigue.

"Well before dawn, I returned to my apartment to prepare. They dressed me in sumptuous clothes. Over

BRUNOR

my veil, they placed a crown of gold and precious stones. I needed to honor the city, the king, and the Frankish people.

"Hardly had the day dawned when the procession left the palace of the Porta Basilica. During the night, in spite of the cold, the people had gathered along the streets leading to the cathedral. We moved through the surging acclamations of the crowd.

"At the head of the procession came the cross. Then Clovis moved forward, led by Remigius, his father in faith. I walked behind them, holding Thierry's hand. My little adopted prince was also going to be baptized. My sisters-in-law followed, then the nobles and the crowd of Franks. Alternating choruses of clergymen started singing joyous Christmas and baptismal hymns.

"The procession came to a stop at the cathedral. Remigius turned toward the crowd, and there was silence. He then asked the ritual question: 'What do you ask of the Church?' 'Baptism!' replied the king. Both voices resounded strongly in the cold air.

"The baptistery enclosure was just big enough to hold our family. Braziers filled with sweet-smelling herbs spread a mild warmth. The illumination was prodigious: thousands of candles, candelabras, and torches shone as if it were broad daylight. Veils, wall-hangings, and clerical vestments were all in white and gold.

"When asked to do so by the bishop, Clovis affirmed his faith by reciting the Credo. Then he moved toward the baptismal font. He stepped slowly, undressed, into the water of purification. I noticed that he had kept on his chains of amber and gold.

"The most solemn moment had arrived. Emotion blurred my vision. I dropped to my knees. I heard Remigius' voice, so clear in the sudden silence. "Bend down your head, Sicamber,[1] and remove your amulets! Burn what you have worshipped and worship what you have burned." Then, extending his hand, the bishop poured the scented water three times onto the king's long hair, naming each person of the Trinity. Overcome, I suddenly saw my husband next to me, completely dressed in white. I raised my hands in a transport of joy, and, forgetting all reserve, I thanked God aloud and asked him to pour out upon his royal disciple a profusion of graces.

"In the packed cathedral, incense was burning in silver vessels. I did not let go of Clovis' hand during the ceremony. Marvelous music brought my happiness to a climax: singers, who had come specially from Milan, made truly celestial choruses ring out. The building vibrated, shimmering with a thousand flames. Clovis was moved: I heard him ask Remigius if these were already the heavenly delights that had been promised to him!

"The remainder of the day was spent in feasting.

[1] The Sicambri were a Germanic people established in the Rhur valley. Some of the Sicambri settled in Gaul, where in the third century A.D. they mixed with the Franks. —TRANS.

Many of our warriors had been baptized. The people, showered with gifts, celebrated with them.

"At the palace, the rejoicing was quieter. Remigius and I exchanged looks full of pride. We had been answered, magnificently, on this day blessed above all others.

"Since that day, dear Injuriosus, that pure and profound joy has been preserved, even in the darkest of times."

"Such an honor is enough to fill a lifetime. The dark times have flown away. Joy remains for eternity."

VI

That night I had a dream about Clodomir, that child whose birth gave us such joy. He was armed for battle, and his blond curls were sticky with blood. My heart torn, I was looking at this dear son. He was staring back at me sadly. "In the name of the living God, I begged him, speak, what do you want?" He answered, "Mother, pray constantly for me. I have committed a great crime." I realized that his soul was not at peace because of the murder of Sigismond!

At the death of my uncle Gondebaud, my sons broke the alliance with Burgundy. They attacked my cousin Sigismond of Burgundy. The land of my birth seemed easy prey to them. Defeated and taken prisoner by Clodomir, Sigismond was thrown into a well along with his wife and children.

The victor should have remembered a warning from the abbot of Micy: "Kill Sigismond, and you will perish. Spare him, and God will protect you." Divine vengeance was swift! It was my sons' turn to be defeated. The victors paraded Clodomir's head on a pike.

I assured my son of my prayers. I would ask for the

intercession of George, patron of horsemen, of Martin, who was an officer, and of Maurice, the soldier-martyr who is venerated in my country. Then the darkness disappeared, and I awoke in tears.

My sons ended by annexing Burgundy, which their father had respected. One day, however, Clovis had to lead his army there, as Godegisile had asked him to come there to rescue him from his brother Gondebaud. I did not involve myself in that conflict, which ended in fratricide. Gondebaud killed Godegisile, and then he wanted to make peace with the Franks. Clovis asked me to join him in Auxerre, where the reconciliation was to take place. I departed reluctantly. I made some short stops along the way on the pretext that I was pregnant. I no longer remember where, but I attended a trial submitted to God's judgment. Accused of murder, a Frankish man had not found among his close relations enough witnesses ready to swear to his innocence. So a fight took place, and the accuser quickly overcame his adversary.

The bishops condemn this form of justice. In general, they are amazed at our German laws, to put it mildly. I have heard people burst out laughing because the Salic Law of the Franks allows the guilty party to pay for damages. They can even pay for the death of a man or for a woman's honor! One of my attendants accused a nobleman of the court of having pressed against her arm when turning a corner of a hallway. The husband had refused any conciliation. Given the rank of the parties involved, the trial was presided over by the king. Clovis restrained his smile. He feared that the affair could turn into a vendetta. The man maintained that he had brushed against the woman because of carelessness and because of the narrowness of the place. They argued for a long time in order to determine if the contact was made by the wrist, the elbow, or the shoulder, a matter of an aggravating circumstance. Finally, the king's comrade was sentenced to pay thirty gold sous to the family of my lady-in-waiting. To some, the verdict seemed severe. I, on the other hand, hoped that it would discourage excess familiarity and would encourage men to show us more respect.

I did not see my uncle in Auxerre, and that pleased me. The alliance had been signed before my arrival. I stayed in the bishop's palace, from which I could look out over the jumble of rooftops as far as the port on the river Yonne. I said my prayers at the tomb of Bishop Germain. I remembered that, when he had been traveling on his way to Nanterre, he had discerned the vocation of Geneviève, who was a child at the time. I decided to have a basilica built in his honor.

Clovis informed me of the reason for his reconciliation with Gondebaud. The latter feared the ambitions of the Visigoths. In addition, their kingdom was blocking Frankish expansion toward the south. Alaric, the Visigoth king, made the mistake of intensifying the repression of Catholics. Even the bishops, among them the famous Caesarius of Arles, were being persecuted.

The clergy urged Clovis to intervene, and I backed them to the greatest of my ability.

Clovis was not a man to act impulsively. The powerful king of the Ostrogoths backed his son-in-law Alaric. The Franks must not fight on two fronts. But as soon as my husband obtained the emperor's backing, he shifted into action.

I had wished for this war against heretical persecutors, and I wanted to observe the departure of our warriors. The dukes and counts had summoned the freemen to Soissons. They arrived animated by a tremendous joy. From childhood, the Franks truly have a passion for war! They do not know fear. Only death can defeat them. But did they consider only death? They imagined the sharing of booty and the glory of victory. Clovis could count on them. They would rather be killed on the spot than flee.

The troops lined up at the sound of the trumpets. I admired their orderliness. During their long period as auxiliaries of the Romans, the Franks had adopted discipline while at the same time preserving their ancestral spirit.

At the head came the king astride the warhorse that was going to save his life in the battle. A pale, spring sun drew flashes of light on his golden shield. The noblemen, all richly outfitted, surrounded him.

Foot soldiers followed in leather boots, with their hair piled high above their shaved necks, their short cloaks flowing over bright-colored jerkins and their legs protected by leggings. I saw few defensive weapons, but there were swords, barbed spears with their two hooks, and above all the terrible battle-ax, so feared by the enemy because its spinning flight reached its mark without fail. These arms are of excellent quality, for the blacksmiths in the north of Gaul make steel of great repute.

Tribe by tribe, the Franks passed by. From far off, we could hear their songs and clamor. Then came the troops that Clovis had raised from among the men of this country. He alone, of all the kings, had dared to do this. These soldiers moved forward, breast-plated and helmeted, a drab mass, after the brightly colored mob. We could hear only the pounding of boots and the brief commands of their leaders.

The spectators around me were very excited. "The Visigoths will be crushed!" they declared. "They have grown much too soft from the easy life of the south; they will not be able to resist us!" They envied those who were going to pillage rich countries. But they suddenly lowered their voices. "The king has forbidden pillage, but that order is against tradition!" "No", someone corrected, "pillage is not forbidden, it is only limited. The persons and property of the Church must not be touched, especially in the area of Tours and Poitiers. In those places no more than grass and water may be taken." They agreed: blessed Martin and blessed Hilary must be protected.

I had confidence in the success of our troops, who

were fighting for a just cause. Days went by. Then one evening, horsemen jumped from their horses beneath my windows. Cries of joy burst forth. My heart leaped, and I rushed out. I saw three young officers who had arrived at a gallop opening up a path for themselves through the enthusiastic crowd. One of them was Thierry. He had been granted the favor of bringing the news that was to give me so much pleasure. The messengers were dust-covered, exhausted, and very excited. Their report seemed confused at times, since the three kept interrupting each other.

According to them, the army had arrived at Tours without encountering any difficulties. But Theudebald explained that they camped some distance from the holy city. Bertramn had been impressed by the exceptionally severe discipline. For having taken wheat from a peasant, one soldier had been put to death in front of the troops. Clovis had said to Thierry, who was begging for leniency: "And where will there be hope of victory if we offend holy Martin?"

I asked my stepson if the king had in fact sent gifts to the blessed man. He said Yes, that Bertramn had been among those carrying the gifts.

"We returned beaming", he informed me. "At the very moment we entered the basilica, the choir was singing 'For you girded me with strength for the battle; you made my assailants sink under me.' Was this not a most favorable sign?"

"The king took it as such", added Thierry, "and in

the blink of an eye, the word spread throughout the army. We were all filled with enthusiasm."

"Fortunately!" exclaimed Theudebald in turn. "Because we were going to need it! Beginning the following morning, the rain started to fall, more and more violently."

"But where were the Visigoths?", we asked.

"Having crossed the Loire," answered Thierry, "we were in enemy territory! And with the weather against us. The earth was soaked; we were advancing with difficulty; we did not arrive at Vienne until evening."

". . . To find", added Theudebald, "that the bridges were destroyed! To make matters worse, the storm had flooded the river fords. Our scouts could not find them. It was necessary to camp on the swampy banks! But at least the water from heaven had stopped falling."

Then all three fell silent and looked at each other. Finally Bertramn took on a mysterious air. "Just before dawn, a ford was finally located. The rumor circulated that a doe had led us to it."

"It is an absolute fact", exclaimed Theudebald. "Heaven sent her to us. Our beloved holy men were surely protecting the army."

It was Thierry who finally told us about the battle. "We met the enemy army a little north of Poitiers, in an area called Vouillé. Then what great blows were exchanged! Always at the front, Clovis was searching for Alaric. When he found him, he killed him in single combat. It was a magnificent joust. But when Alaric

BRUNOR

was on the ground, his guard rushed our vanquisher. But Clovis' horse saved the king by suddenly stepping to one side."

We all congratulated one another. Heaven had saved the one who was fighting on its side.

By now, the Visigoths were fleeing toward their lands in Spain, and our people were pursuing them.

"Long live the Christ who loves the Franks", my chaplain concluded.

"Was the fighting very bloody?" asked one of my ladies. She had several sons in the army. There was a silence, which I broke by inviting the gathering to go to chapel. We should give thanks to God and pray for the dead.

That victory made the Franks masters of the west as far as the Pyrenees mountains. The army established its winter headquarters in Bordeaux. My husband asked me to go there. I left with our children, and I settled in the residence of Bishop Cyprien. I took a liking to that large city, which was still so marked by memories of the Romans. I liked to stroll on the banks of the Garonne, above all when the tide rolled upriver, bringing with it the scent of the sea.

In the springtime, Clovis continued on to Toulouse the campaign that had begun so well.

Polin, the new governor of Bordeaux, invited me to his villa at Bazas. The month spent in that residence seemed like a day. I had never known such a gentle way of life. The region itself was full of charm. There were nothing but vine-covered rolling hills everywhere. My eyes were filled with that landscape where the river moved lazily through the fruit trees. The curves of the horizon were interrupted by tall cypress trees, which made it even more agreeable by contrast.

As for the house, or rather the palace, everything there was sumptuous and comfortable, in the style of rich Romans. Forty rooms were arranged around the numerous courtyards. My apartment looked out over a garden with a portico. It was magnificently ornamented. The walls were covered in green and white marble; the floor was paved in mosaic and covered with thick carpets. In the evenings it was heated, despite the mildness of the weather. But it seemed to me that the height of comfort was the suite of thermal baths, also luxuriously decorated with marble and mosaics.

The villa kept a studio for mosaic artists. The children loved that place. They would watch the skillful hands reproduce the design from a large oriental carpet that hung on the wall. I had to prevent them from taking hold of the brilliant little cubes and from walking on blocks of mortar ready to receive the pieces of glass.

To get back to Bordeaux, we went down the Garonne aboard a small pleasure boat pulled by slaves. A pavilion made of drapery protected us from the sun and wind. We were served a light meal of oysters from the nearby ponds, as famous as the wine that accompanied them.

Clovis returned from Toulouse in triumph. He brought back with him the legendary Visigoth treasure. He set about organizing what he had conquered. That left him little spare time for his family. Our little Clothilde complained of rarely seeing her father, who nevertheless loved her dearly.

That year, everything seemed to favor my husband. Emperor Anastasius of Constantinople rewarded his ally with the title of Consul. One piece of good fortune never arrives alone. We learned from a letter sent by Avitus that Gondebaud had converted. He and his people were finally becoming Catholic.

On the route northward, we made a stop at Tours. It was there that Anastasius' ambassadors joined us. They brought to the king the official document from the emperor's diploma. The city had gone to great expense. We ourselves had dressed in our most sumptuous attire. We wanted to match the height of the imperial splendor of Byzantium.

In front of the basilica, Clovis received the lordly delegation. The consular document was contained in a precious coffer made of ivory. The king then mounted his horse. He wore a purple tunic, to which his rank of consul entitled him, a gold-embroidered mantle around his shoulders, a diadem around his long hair. All along the road, he threw gold coins to the crowd. It was truly a triumph worthy of the ancient Romans. In Tours, they remember it still.

We arrived in Paris in the winter. At the south gate, the city's notables, muffled up in furs, were waiting for us. The people, stamping their feet in the snow, were shouting "Noël!" Clovis had decided to make

Paris his capital. Without ever having the brilliance of Lyon, Lutetia had received emperors, above all Constantine, who had also converted to Christianity and whom the king took as a model.

Now gathered within its walls and sheltered on its island, Paris still had its prestigious memories. We settled into the former palace of the governors at the westward tip of the isle. Flattered at our choice of their city, the Parisians offered us processions and banquets where they mingled with us.

Geneviève, alas, was gone. With her small community, I went to pray at her simple tomb. No foreboding gripped me. Little did I know, when I climbed Mount Lutetia that first time, that three years later I was to bury my human happiness there.

VII

While I was strolling in the garden before vespers, rapid footsteps caused the gravel behind me to crunch. I turned around, and for a moment I thought I saw young Clovis coming toward me out of the past. But it was only his grandson, Théodebert, son of Thierry, who had also died at an early age.

In order to see me, the king of Austrasia had made a detour on his way to Auvergne. On seeing and hearing him, I felt both pleasure and pain.

In contrast to his grandfather, Théodebert speaks willingly and expresses himself well. He recalls his voyages as far as Provence, where I would so like to have gone, and also his battles, and a chariot race over which he presided in the amphitheater at Arles. Having caused the revival of this sport beloved of the Greeks and Romans seems to give him his greatest pride!

In the half-light of my cell to which he has taken me back, I let myself be lulled to sleep by the mysterious similarity of his voice. The words, in themselves, are unimportant. It is Clovis speaking to me again. The voice suddenly stops. Then Théodebert is asking me if I am unwell. And I become aware that I have forgotten the duties of hospitality. Wine is brought to my guest, served in a precious crystal cup. It came from Alaric's treasure. I keep it as a reminder of Vouillé.

The prince suddenly extracts a gold coin from his purse and gives it to me. My vision is no longer good, but I do not mistake it. He has had his own effigy struck on the coin. He has dared to replace the image of the emperor with his own. Théodebert seems amused at my astonishment.

"The venerable queen seems shocked! But why?"

"But what will the emperor think?" I protest.

"But who is the emperor here", he exclaims, "if not those kings descended from Clovis? "In any case, be assured! Everything is fine between the emperor and me. We send each other many messages. My scribes write an excellent Latin."

He leans over, kisses my hand, and gets up to leave. I hand him the cup that he so much admired, saying, "Take it with you, it is worthy of the one who wants to be the only emperor in his kingdom."

He laughs and leaves delighted, unaware of the sumptuous gift he has just given to me: a moment of life, of lightheartedness, of youth.

Radegonde enters, seeming exhausted. She has just spent hours with the sick at the hospital. I insist that she rest; I have her sit down next to me. I tell her about my conversation with Théodebert. So like Clovis! And yet so different! In spite of his fire and ambition, will he ever experience his ancestor's glory? And yet my husband's life was cut short. How many plans were crushed by his unexpected death!

When he established himself in Paris, Clovis was in the prime of life. He was incredibly active. At first he occupied himself with his new capital in order to create a city worthy of a sovereign of the Gauls. I fell in love right away with that city and its river. I imagined a brilliant future for her.

From my window, I had a view of Mount Lutetia, her vineyards, and her cemetery, where Geneviève was resting. And if one day that mount were to have Geneviève's name? Then it was that I suggested that my husband build for our friend a tomb worthy of her. But he did better than that. He wanted to construct a basilica there on the site of the ancient temple of Jupiter. Like the one at Constantinople where they buried the emperors, he would dedicate it to the holy apostles, and we, too, would have our burial place there.

For the king, a plan needed to be implemented immediately. So the building site was opened, and crowds of artisans hurried there, happy to escape the idleness to which the problems of the time were reducing them.

To my surprise, Clovis wanted the foundations of the monument to be solemnized with a pagan ceremony.

That day, a long procession climbed up the road of the mount. Warrior songs were mixed with hymns in that strange ceremony that was both pagan and Christian.

At the designated place, an area had been set aside. Trumpets sounded. Clovis moved forward alone. Facing the rising sun, he lifted his battle-ax and threw it some distance. By doing this, he took possession of the area. Fortunately, few of us understood the significance of that ancestral gesture by which our forebears placed themselves under the protection of the god Thor, the thrower of thunderbolts.

Then the clergy advanced to bless the site. Christ had the last word.

Today the basilica compares favorably with its imperial model. Parisians are proud of it. They refer to it simply as "Geneviève's church". They give Clovis and Clothilde a share in the respectful affection they give to their patroness.

Clovis was never to see more than the foundations of the structure. He was forty-five, and he seemed strong when a violent illness carried him off. That year, November had been particularly cold. The old palace was difficult to heat, and an icy humidity rose from the Seine.

On the feast day of blessed Martin, the king did not appear in church. He had returned soaked from a day of hunting. I hurried to his bedside. Raised up on a number of cushions, Clovis was breathing with difficulty between bouts of coughing. The physicians found his pulse rapid. But they were not excessively

worried for they were familiar with the robust constitution of the patient. Kept in a warm place, my husband was to drink strong herbal teas. He seemed to improve. He wanted to receive a messenger from the emperor. Too soon, it seems. He caught cold again. Above all, a great fatigue, the result of years of incessant work, swept down on him. The fever returned worse than ever. Soon the king became delirious. I sent for a Jewish physician, famous in that city. He let it be known that he was being called very late. He applied cupping glasses, and the best of leeches. All effort was in vain. Then the bishop came to anoint the king with holy oil. I did not fully realize my misfortune until I saw my husband on his bier and the soldiers marching past him in silence while priests chanted psalms. In public, I held back my tears. I had the strength to lead the funeral cortège. At the Basilica of the Holy Apostles, we passed under scaffolding to reach the crypt. I could no longer contain my grief. Then I found a kind of solace in cutting my hair and placing it on the winding sheet. The body was placed in a sarcophagus ornamented simply with a cross. Not far from there, a lamp was burning at Geneviève's tomb. I turned toward her and prayed ardently, asking her to intercede for the one who was about to meet his judge.

To my sorrow was added a serious disappointment. My sons, still adolescents, proceeded to break up the kingdom without consulting me. However, I yielded and hid my distress.

I gave up the island palace to Childebert, who had

become the king of Paris. I retired to the Thermes palace at the foot of Mount Lutetia. It was closer to the basilica. In any case, I preferred that semi-rural residence.

Childebert proved to be respectful. He was cultivated and could speak about something other than dogs, horses, and weapons. But his visits were rare and brief. At those times, the courtyard and vestibule resounded with the noise of a boisterous and impatient retinue. One day I complained:

"Son, have I become a stranger to you?"

"Mother", he answered, "I arose well before dawn, and I went to bed late. I have to compel the recognition of men older than I am."

"But they have to obey the son of Clovis", I protested.

"The mere remembrance of my father will not preserve their fidelity to me. So forgive me if my activities do not permit me to enjoy your presence more."

Such was his answer, and I considered the matter closed. I began to reproach myself for not having been closer to my children, of having been more wife than mother. I realized what my mission from then on was to be: to act through prayer. And I found ample material about which to pray for my sons. As very young kings, they let themselves be guided by counselors without scruples. They were giving free rein to their ancestral violence. As for Christianity, they only participated in the rituals.

My daughter, Clothilde, stayed close by me. She resembled me without having my vitality. Sweet and dreamy, she grew flowers, raised turtledoves and would often sit embroidering with her cats at her feet. Having her mother all to herself gave her some consolation for the loss of her beloved father. However, I came to worry about her extreme sensitivity. It was necessary to keep her from glimpsing groups of prisoners. She refused to attend punishments that the law inflicts. She suffered over the fate of slaves. Even the hunt was unbearable to her. Her tender and peaceful soul was out of harmony with this pitiless world. I thought of placing her within the shelter of a cloister. It was somewhat with her in mind that I founded the monastery where I now live.

One day my youngest son, Clothaire, left Soissons, his capital city, to pay me a visit. He so furiously reproached me for living in Paris that I almost raised my hand against him. I had not made such a gesture since, as a child, I had struck a servant woman and had incurred the severe reproaches of my mother.

Clothaire pretended to see in my choice of residence a sign of preference for Childebert. He claimed that his filial affection had been wounded. The indecipherable look of his sea-green eyes put me ill at ease. I ended by lowering my own in front of that adolescent boy. I guessed his true fear: his brother might take advantage of the respect I enjoyed among the people. Since I wanted peace, I agreed to move to Tours. That city, situated in Clodomir's kingdom, had belonged to me since my marriage. With my daughter, I spent peaceful years there. We loved the religious character of Martin's city, its processions and the sound of its bells. I showered the basilica with gifts and transformed wooden churches everywhere into stone edifices.

I thought a great deal then of keeping my daughter near me. But misfortune arrived one day with a messenger from my sons. They informed me that from far-off Spain, Amalaric, king of the Visigoths, was asking for their sister in marriage. For once in agreement, they did not doubt my approval. That alliance would cover the kingdom to the south. And, I foresaw, it could one day be a pretext for military intervention. For the ambitions of my sons were as insatiable as those of their father.

I could not deny that the union was honorable. On the other hand, I could not get used to the idea of sending my daughter far away; she was so helpless, so delicate. And above all to marry the man whose father Clovis had killed! I remained several days in uncertainty. Finally I gathered up all my courage to talk with Clothilde. She threw herself into my arms, crying. "Mother, if it is possible, keep me here with you."

"My daughter", I said to her, "it is with great sorrow that I will see you leave. But just imagine that this marriage might possibly convert the Visigoths. Like your mother, you could be God's instrument." The princess then no longer resisted. That perspective marked out for her where her duty lay.

A sumptuous procession took the sister of four powerful kings, the daughter of the great Clovis, to Spain.

I myself travelled to Toulouse, through regions where peace had brought prosperity. Clothilde was silent. I tried to force myself to be cheerful. I tried to comfort my child and to instill in her my energy. But when the curtain of her carriage fell again over the hand that she had been waving as though calling for help, I was overcome with apprehension. I was considered unreasonable. There were whispers that I was getting old. At every stop, had I not received a reassuring message? But at the border, the Frankish escort was sent back. Even her own ladies-in-waiting were refused entry. From then on, I received only rare and official-sounding letters from my daughter.

I notified Clodomir about it, but he did not take my fears seriously. "Why", he wrote to me, "would they mistreat such a beautiful and sweet person? And how would they dare fail to show consideration toward the daughter and sister of Frankish kings?"

So I kept my worries to myself. Years passed. Until the arrival of a message from Childebert. He happened to be in the Auvergne when a monk coming from Spain had passed on to him a call for help from his sister. She was living in a hell, spied on, insulted, and even struck whenever she wished to go to church. A blood-soaked cloth attested to this. Childebert had immediately set off on a campaign to Spain. Amalaric, defeated, paid with his life for the outrage done to the Franks. My son brought Clothilde out, but in what a state! She died on the way back. We buried her near her father. Beneath her sweet head, I placed a cushion of flowers. I entrusted her, also, to Geneviève.

Having returned to Tours, I committed myself to making that city an oasis of peace in memory of my daughter. The people gave me credit for this. The Lord God must have looked favorably on my work, because he was about to ask me for the greatest proof of love, that proof which distinguishes the true Christian, forgiveness for what is humanly unforgivable.

VIII

About that memory, I can speak only to God in my prayers. I am still praying for my criminal sons, and also for myself, because I was unable to protect my grandchildren.

hen Clodomir was killed, Clothaire took possession of his brother's widow. Indignant, I demanded the couple's three children. They were ten, seven, and five years old. I dedicated all my strength and love to their education. Those princes would truly be Christian princes, new Constantines.

I moved back into the Thermes palace under the protection of Childebert. I tried to interest my son in his nephews. I would take them to him and praise them to him. That tortured mind ended by bearing them a grudge because of the affection that I had for them. Then the monstrous idea sprouted and grew in his mind to do away with them. He dared not act alone, however. So he suggested to Clothaire that they be accomplices. The young nephews to be eliminated, so cherished by their grandmother, would never seek their paternal heritage.

Clothaire was without scruples. He came running,

and the plot was hatched. Of these schemes, I had no idea. I pursued my peaceful life, trusting in the king's kindness as though I had never known the knavery of the court. How could one imagine such infamy?

With what joy I was fulfilling my role as grandmother. Everything in the palace revolved about the children: lessons for the older ones with tutors and riding masters; games for the youngest one with the nursemaid and governess; visits from physicians.

I was still young and strong at that time. In all kinds of weather, I would take them for walks. We would climb to the basilica. They particularly liked the autumn trips to the vineyards because the scarecrow slaves would flap their arms to scare away the birds. Or instead, we would cross over the little wooden bridge and enter the city, where everything was a spectacle for my boys. There were storytellers, jugglers, singers, strolling merchants, artisans working in public. Their favorites were the armorers.

Never had Childebert been nicer. I did not see danger approaching.

That particular day, the weather was clear and cold. Théodebald and Gonthier were playing not far from me. Clodoald was sleeping, tired from the walk.

The court usher announced a messenger from the king. It was Anslebert, a former vassal for Clovis, to whom he had been entrusted when quite young as a page. He was unaware of the real reason for his mission, but my sons knew that this faithful man would inspire my confidence. After greeting me, he asked me to hand over the children to him, for the kings wanted to crown them. My first inclination was the correct one. I was worried about this excessive rush, and I asked for a delay so I could prepare myself to accompany the princes.

Anslebert stated that the haste was due to the short time that the king of Soissons had at his disposal, as he had to return as soon as possible to his capital. I then reproached myself for my distrust. My sons were at last showing themselves in a better light.

I summoned the older two. Their long hair had been combed and they were dressed in their finest clothes. I had them given something to eat, and I personally wrapped woolens around their necks. Anslebert was growing impatient. The children kissed me quickly and left joyfully in the midst of their escort. I can see them still . . .

I then busied myself with the youngest. I berated the servants. We had to act quickly. The child, half-asleep, was whimpering. His nurse scolded him. He must behave, he was going to have a beautiful golden crown . . .

I ordered my litter to be brought immediately. Then an uproar broke out in the hall. A man rushed into my rooms, followed by the usher in a state of panic. I recognized Arcadius. That noble Roman was the grandson of Sidonius, my parents' dinner guest. He had taken from the barbarians, whom his grandfather despised, not only his dress but also the crudest of manners. I did not regard him highly, as he was one of those who encouraged my sons in their extravagance so he could take advantage of them.

I saw him brandishing scissors in one hand and a sword in the other. I did not even have time to be shocked by his audacity. "A message from the kings", he shouted. Then he changed to an oily voice to say to me, "Glorious Queen! Your sons, our lords, are letting you decide: What is to be done with the children? Should we cut their hair and let them live, or should we kill them? You decree!"

Death could be no worse than what I felt at that moment. I thought my blood was draining out of me. My heart stopped beating. My sight blurred. As in a nightmare where one's paralyzed body is trying in vain to flee, I tried to stifle the ghastly words that, in spite of myself, came out of my mouth. What pride, what confusion dominated me at that instant? To this day, I still do not know. "I would rather they be dead than clipped." I had actually pronounced those accursed words! Arcadius carried off those words in haste. Then I came out of my paralysis and shouted orders to the horror-stricken servants. The miserable man was already far away. Anslebert, despairing, later told me about the horrible scene. Childebert had yielded to the pleas of his nephews, who were crawling at the feet of their uncle. But Clothaire reminded him of his role as instigator and even resorted to threatening him. The coward then permitted the crime to be committed.

Clothaire cleared out, and Childebert became invisible. I took advantage of this in order to save Clodoald.

Devoted servants carried him away to the monastery of Chelles, and he was later hidden in other abbeys.

In the snow, all Paris attended the funeral procession for my little children. Once again I held back my tears, having consideration for the rank of the murderers. Then I gathered together my household, divided among my servants the riches from my coffers, and freed the remainder of my slaves. I sent everyone away, keeping with me only a few intimate friends. The seneschal, the senior officer of the royal court, pointed out to me that the queen could not do without a large entourage. I answered him that the queen was dead. From then on, I would be only a servant in blessed Martin's basilica. I returned to Tours for good.

After a year, in the summertime, I felt strong enough to travel. In short stages, I went by litter toward the hamlet of Nogent, near Paris. We passed by Chelles, one of the monasteries I had founded. The old nuns still remembered Clodoald's arrival there, the little boy's tears, his calls for his grandmother, and his refusal to respond to the new name intended to protect him. The nuns had consoled him, surrounded him with affection, but when the child had to leave again, it meant tearing him away again. I prayed often that Clodoald would not be found; later, I prayed that he would not seek vengeance. But he chose to embrace the life of the monks who had raised him. Now, he lives as a hermit in the forest that borders Paris on the west. It is he that I wished to see again.

We circled around the city. In Nogent, a peasant

pointed to the clearing where "the man of God" lived. Clovis' grandson lived in a hut near a spring. I found him lying prostrate before a wooden crucifix. Leaving my escort at the edge of the trees, I approached, barely daring to disturb his meditation.

Along the way, I had prepared for our meeting, what I would say, what I would do . . . When Clodoald raised toward me the same clear-eyed look as Geneviève had had and welcomed me with that same kindly smile, I dropped to my knees. Then it was that I poured out all the tears that I had held back for such a long time. It was my grandson who had taken me in his arms.

"God will wipe away every tear from their eyes", he said to me, so speaks the Lord in the Apocalypse. "Realize that my brothers are close to God. They have escaped the temptations of the world. As for me, Christ has given me the grace of calling me to his exclusive service. Thus have I chosen freely what had at first been imposed upon me. I have offered up to God my offended pride and my desire for vengeance. Now I have been able to forgive."

"So you, too, have forgiven!" I murmured. He answered, "Yes, both of us have forgiven those wretched beings. We are praying for them, are we not?"

"Now", he added with authority, "there remains but one, last, and important forgiveness to be granted. It is the one you owe to yourself."

I felt these words penetrate my heart. Mysteriously, I was being freed of my shackles. "God is speaking

through you. Blessed is he for having inspired these words of release." Thus did I thank my grandson who helped me find peace again.

I am confident that in the accounting of the final judgment, the life of Clodoald will weigh more than the crimes of his family.[1]

What a mystery is the intercession with God by the saints who loved him more than anything! I think back to that night of agony which I went through eight years ago. A messenger, having arrived at full gallop, had told me that war had broken out between my sons. When attacked by Childebert, Clothaire had taken refuge in the forest of Brotonne. His situation appeared desperate. Would the cup of family hatred never cease to be filled? Would I have to weep over the murder of a brother after that of innocent children? In my name, the governor of Tours had sent men to intervene with my two sons. I doubted that they could arrive in time. Then I begged heaven, through the intercession of Martin, our protector.

Night had fallen when I hastened to the basilica with some nuns. We crossed the deserted courtyard, and we heard the pilgrims settling in for the night in cells all around. I had the doors opened, and we entered. In the half-light, I walked toward Martin's tomb behind the altar. There, a perpetual light was burning. I bowed low, placing my head on the cold marble slab. Then I stretched out, despite the protests of the nuns.

[1] Clodoald became a saint, known in English as Saint Cloud.—Trans.

All night long, our prayers rose upward. Day arrived, causing the gold on the mosaics and paintings to blaze forth. Frescoes of the life of the blessed one emerged slowly from the darkness. Candles were lit around the tall columns. In a haze of weariness, I could just make out the incessant parade of pilgrims, who, in every language were invoking the kindly patron of that place. A long line of infirm people tramped along in order to touch the tomb; some dragged themselves along on the marble pavement. A peasant, clothed in sackcloth and with bare feet, asked for a little oil from the tomb lamp in order to nurse his cow. Two poor creatures were secretly cutting off ends of the bell rope as minor relics. Sunday Mass began. I let myself be lulled by the hymns. Two groups of choristers were responding to one another. It is I who founded their school. Beautiful singing helps us to pray.

Shouts suddenly disturbed my meditation. They spread into an uproar outside. People around us had seen an adolescent boy suddenly cured of his paralysis. He had been coming there every day for three years. His perseverance has been rewarded.

My fatigue having completely disappeared, I ordered that he be brought to me. In that cure I saw a sign: I was sure of being heard. The returning messengers confirmed it. A terrible storm had struck Childebert's army. The hail was so strong that the soldiers had had to cover themselves with their shields. But the storm spared the clearing where Clothaire had taken refuge. Childebert retreated. Even my terrible sons knew how to recognize the manifestations of divine power! Besides, it was only with reluctance that their soldiers were following them. The Franks do not like to fight other Franks. After the miracle, they must have put pressure on their chiefs.

Radegonde enters joyfully. "I am unable to go to town without hearing your good deeds praised. Even today", she continues, "when I was leaving the basilica, a musician came up to me. He wanted news of you, having learned that you were unwell. His name is Gerhadt."

I tell my daughter-in-law how God had literally placed this man on the road I was traveling. During a journey, years ago, my coach had passed a limping man accompanied by a young boy. Both seemed sad and weary. I ordered the coachman to stop, and I leaned out to call to them. They remained motionless, visibly frightened in spite of the man's hunting spear and the youngster's cutlass. They eventually came near. Despite the reproachful look from my maid, I had them climb up next to me. On the road, the man told me his story. He was a Frank who farmed a small field on the north bank of the Loire. He had been wounded in one of King Clovis' campaigns. Hampered by his handicap and having to provide for a large family, he had been unable to cope with a series of poor harvests. He had found it necessary to sell his farm animals and then send his plough and a few jewels, undoubtedly the fruit of some bygone pillage, to the usurer. And then finally, he had had to part with his weapons. He considered himself diminished, incapable as he was of presenting himself at the review of freemen on the Field of Mars. Then he had resigned himself to go beg for help from a big landowner of that area. It was not with a merry heart that he, a Frank and a freeman, was on his way to make himself a dependent of another man. His son was accompanying him in order to serve as a witness to the contract, and he would receive a slap, which, better than any words, would cause him to remember the business. Then the man concluded sadly, "But it is I who will be the most humiliated."

In my alms bag, I took a handful of coins: "You have met the widow of Clovis. In his name, you, who were his soldier, accept this from me. It will be enough to free you from your debts." And I added: "Pray to God for the kings who are Clovis' sons. Do you want to entrust your child to me? He pleases me, and I will assure his future."

"So you allowed him to become a singer for the glory of God and his family to escape the shame of misery. You will not be easily forgotten, above all in Tours", Radegonde assures. "In any case, rejoice", she lets out happily, "you are going to have a historiographer!"

She laughs at my astonishment. "It is the nephew of the bishop of Clermont; you know, little Grégoire, that well-behaved child who accompanied his uncle when he came to visit you. He declared when he left that he would one day tell the life of the noble Clothilde. And even the history of the Franks!"

I do remember that child. I was struck by his seriousness and by the attention with which he listened to us run through our memories. He might have been eight or ten years old. His uncle wants to make a bishop of him. In that case, he will have many other things to think about besides writing the life of a former queen![2]

But of what importance is fame among men? "Vanity of vanities!" says Ecclesiastes. I hand myself over to the Father. I offer him my kingdom, my sons, and the future. I am leaving now toward eternity.

[2] Grégoire, having become the bishop of Tours, wrote the *History of the Franks*, in which he greatly praised Clothilde.

Epilogue

They entered, radiant, holding each other by the hand. Eberhardt was coming to present his fiancée to me. He is a Frank, the count's relative. She is the daughter of a noble Gallo-Roman. Rare in my youth, these unions are increasing in number now, and I rejoice because of it. The young woman speaks Latin mixed with words taken from our own language. Her name is Hildegarde, and she does her chestnut-colored hair in our style and has even adopted the short skirt. The young man gracefully wears the irridescent clothes of the noblemen of his people. He talks about hunting, and she about poetry. But both of them are Catholic, and for the future, only that is important.

Here, beside my bed, a small ivory box holds some treasured souvenirs. From it I remove a gold box, ornamented with pearls and engraved with a cross. I offer it to the young couple, who are a living symbol of the union of two peoples, for which I worked. It contains a precious relic of blessed Martin, the protector of our kingdom. This kingdom that Clovis built. They are more and more numerous, those who live in it and who call themselves Franks, whatever their origins. They all are now or will be Catholics. The

Church has triumphed. I am proud to have assisted in this. I have accomplished my mission. Now I can leave, singing this psalm, "To you, O Lord, I lift up my soul. Come and save us. You are my refuge. When I awake, I shall be satisfied with beholding your form."